KU-229-646

Titles in the Series

® — Honey Bear Books is a trademark owned by
Honey Bear Productions Inc., and is registered
in the U.S. Patent and Trademark Office.
All rights reserved.

Sunshine Books™ is a trademark owned
by Modern Publishing, A Division of
Unisystems, Inc.
© 1986 Text Copyright by Joshua Morris, Inc.
© 1986 Illustrations Copyright by Martspress, Ltd.
All rights reserved.
Printed in Belgium

FAVORITE TOYS

ILLUSTRATED BY MARY BROOKS
TEXT ADAPTED BY JANE RESNICK
AND SUSAN POSTCANSER

Modern Publishing
A Division of Unisystems, Inc.
New York, New York 10022

UPSIDE DOWN

"What's *this* doing on the floor?"
Christopher exclaimed. "I know it
belongs on a shelf. That's where I've
always seen it." Christopher didn't
know what to call it, but he liked the
way it looked. He knew he shouldn't
touch it, but it was too hard to resist.
Christopher picked it up and held it.
Then he put it down.
The best part was inside, but he
couldn't get in there. So Christopher
sat and thought and stared.
The little house underneath the glass
seemed nice and cozy and warm. "It
would be good to live in there,"
Christopher thought. And the weather
would never change. But how would
you know if it were summer or
spring or winter or fall?
The answer lay in Christopher's
hands—until that moment he didn't
know. Then he turned it upside
down, and the whole thing
filled with snow!

MARY BROOKS

BRAND NEW DRUM

Rat-a-tat-tat, rat-a-tat-tum! Timmy loved
to play his brand new drum. He would
bang the drum as loud as he could and
march all over the house. But Timmy
was sometimes sad, because he couldn't
always play when he wanted to.
Mommy would say, "That's enough for
today Timmy, it's time to go to bed."
Timmy tried to wait, he tried ever-so-
hard. But making music was his very
favorite thing. So Timmy would hold
the drum sticks in his hands and beat
them just above the drum. "I'll make
music in the air! Rat-a-tat-tat, rat-a-
tat-tum," he sang all to himself.
Pretending to play, he decided
is almost as much fun!

EVERY MORNING WHEN I WAKE

Every morning when Jenny wakes up,
the first thing she sees is her teddy bear.
He's lying right there beside her. And
everyday they do something together.
Sometimes they go exploring in the
woods nearby. They make up funny
names for flowers and make friends
with fuzzy caterpillars. Sometimes they
go shopping with Mommy and have
lunch at a restaurant.
And when the day is over and
Mommy and Daddy tuck Jenny
into bed at night, she makes sure
her teddy bear is there beside her
and then she feels just right.

THE JACK-IN-THE-BOX

Bobby and his dog, Scottie, are sitting
in the den and up pops Jack-in-the-Box,
Ka-Boom! Scottie is astounded, he
really is afraid. But Bobby laughs
and giggles, he says, "Now, Scottie,
don't be scared. I'm going to play
with my Jack-in-the-Box and I
want you to play along."
So Scottie watches Bobby. He watches
Jack-in-the-Box, too. Jack jumps up
quickly, but Bobby plays with Jack
over and over again. So Scottie
settles down and waits for Bobby
to play with him.

THE DOLL HOUSE

Today is Susie's birthday. She is three
years old. Her older sister Debbie gave
her a big hug and said, "Because it is
your birthday, you may play
with some of my toys!"
Susie chose the doll house. She thought
it was just the perfect thing to play with
on her birthday. She opened it very
carefully and peeked inside. Then she
held up the tiny doll bed and put it in a
corner. "Now it's perfect for a little
baby doll," she said. All of a sudden,
Susie's dog, Bowser, stuck his head
through one of the doll house windows.
"No, Bowser," laughed Susie, "this
doll house is not for you!"
When Susie had everything in order,
she called Debbie over to take a look.
"It's wonderful!" cried Debbie.
"It's never looked so good."
Susie smiled and thought the day
was wonderful, too!

A PROMISE IS A PROMISE

Sally and her teddy bear, Hugs,
were the best of friends. They
played and laughed together from
sun up to sun down.
One day, Sally decided to have a serious
talk with Hugs about promises. Sally
turned to Hugs, and pulled him up
close and whispered, "A promise is a
special thing that only friends can
share. It's how we let each other know
that we'll never let the other one
down. We'll always take care of each
other, won't we Hugs?" Sally knew
Hugs agreed that friendship is
forever. She was glad that her
teddy bear was for keeps.

THE TICK-TOCKING CLOCK

"Tick, tock," said the clock, as Tommy
put it near his ear. Tommy carried a
tiny clock around because he
loved its ticking sound.
One day Tommy and his Daddy passed
a big store, with clocks in the
window and clocks by the door.
"Well, Tommy," said Daddy. "Look
what we've found! A store filled up
with tick-tocking sounds!"
Tommy just smiled and reached in his
pocket. And guess what he found?
His favorite shiny, tiny clock!

BARNEY, THE WORLD'S BEST ELEPHANT

There's nothing quite like a toy elephant to have as a very best friend. They are always in the mood to do whatever you want to do.

Barney is an elephant, and he's the perfect friend. If I just feel like resting, perhaps sitting in my favorite chair, Barney always understands, he's never a mean old grouch.

When I feel like exploring, Barney tags right along. He knows the road into the woods and where all the flowers are.

He makes friends with the chipmunks, and he makes friends with the toads, he even knows where all the magic fairies live!

And because Barney's such a smart elephant, I take Barney with me everywhere I go!